THE MIRACLES OF YOUR MIND

THE MIRACLES OF YOUR MIND

DR. JOSEPH MURPHY

EMBASSY BOOKS
www.embassybooks.in

The Miracles of Your Mind by Dr. Joseph Murphy

This edition first published in 2017

Published in India by:
Embassy Book Distributors
120, Great Western Building,Maharashtra
Chamber of Commerce Lane,
Fort, Mumbai - 400 023.
Tel : (91-22) 22819546 / 22818567.
Email : info@embassybooks.in
Website : www.embassybooks.in

Distribution Centres:
Mumbai, Bangalore, Kolkata, Chennai,
Hyderabad, New Delhi, Pune

ISBN: 978-93-86450-72-2

Page Design and Layout by PSV Kumarasamy

Printed & Bound in India by Printone Solutions, Navi Mumbai

CONTENTS

PUBLISHER'S PREFACE

In this extraordinary book Dr. Murphy reveals the inner workings of the subconscious mind, and makes this book one of the most practical guides in overcoming the troubles that beset mankind. The amazing results, "miracles," some might call them, reported by those who attended Dr. Murphy's lectures on The Miracles of the Subconscious Mind brought hundreds of letters from others who wanted to learn how to tap the infinite power of the subconscious mind. In this book you will find practical techniques for achieving health, wealth, peace, and harmony.

From the chapter on The Subconscious Mind and Health: "In using the subconscious mind you infer no opponent; you use no will power. You use imagination, not will power. You imagine the end and the freedom state. You will find your intellect trying to get in the way, but persist in maintaining a simple, child-like, miracle-making faith. Picture yourself without the ailment or problem. Imagine the emotional accompaniments of the freedom-state you crave. Gut out all of the red tape from the process. The simple way is always the best."

You desire a happier, fuller, and richer life. Begin to use this miracle-working power and smooth your way in daily affairs, solve business problems, and bring harmony in family relationships. Be sure that you read this book several times. Let the author show you in these many chapters how this wonderful power works, and how you can draw out the hidden inspiration and wisdom that is within you. Learn the simple techniques of impressing the subconscious mind. Follow the new, scientific way in tapping the infinite storehouse. Read this book carefully, earnestly, and lovingly. Prove to yourself the amazing way it can help you. It could be the turning point in your life.

CHAPTER 1

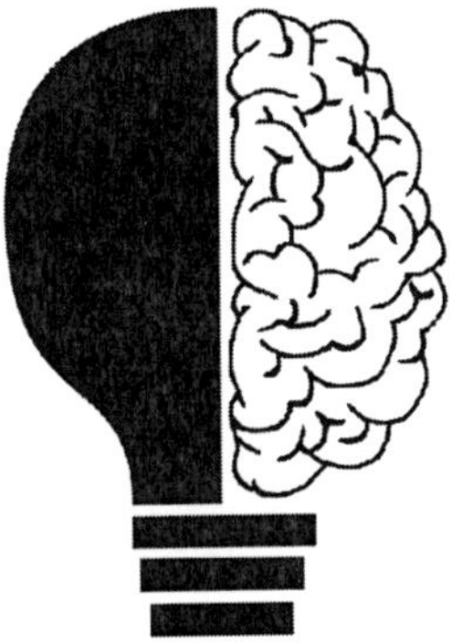

HOW YOUR OWN MIND WORKS

Man has only one mind, but he has two distinct phases or functions of the one mind. Each phase is characterized by its own phenomena which is peculiar to itself. Each of these minds is 0capable of independent action, as well as synchronous action. We call one the objective mind, because it deals with external things, and the other is the subjective mind. The subjective mind is amenable, and controlled by suggestion of the objective or conscious mind. The objective mind takes cognizance of the objective world. The media of observation are the five physical senses. The objective mind is your guide in your contact with the environment. We gain knowledge through the five senses. The objective mind learns through observation, experience, and education. The greatest function of the conscious mind is that of reasoning.

Look around Los Angeles; you come to the conclusion that it is a beautiful city based upon your observation of the parks, the buildings, the beautiful structure, the lovely flower gardens, etc. This is the working of your conscious or objective mind.

The word *objective* means that it deals with objective things. The subjective mind takes cognizance of its environment by means independent of the five physical senses. The subjective mind or the subconscious mind – either term may be used – perceives by intuition. The subconscious mind is the seat of your emotions. We know without a doubt that it performs its highest functions when the objective senses are in abeyance.

It is the intelligence that makes itself manifest when the conscious mind is suspended or in a sleepy, drowsy state. The subconscious mind sees without the use of the eyes; it has the capacity of clairvoyance and clairaudience. The subconscious mind can leave the body; travel to distant lands, and bring back intelligence oftentimes of the most exact and truthful character. Through the subconscious mind you can read the thoughts of others, even to the minutest details; read the contents of sealed envelopes and closed safes.

The subconscious mind has the ability to apprehend the thoughts of others without the use of the ordinary, objective means of communication. So it is of the greatest importance that we understand the interaction of the conscious and subconscious mind, in order to learn the true art of prayer.

Now there are many terms used in describing the objective and the subjective mind. They are, as we told you, called: The conscious or subconscious mind, the waking or sleeping mind, the surface self or the deep self, voluntary mind or involuntary mind, the male and the female, and many other terms. Remember there is only one mind having two phases or functions.

The subjective mind is always amenable to suggestion; it is controlled by suggestion. We must recognize that the subconscious mind accepts all suggestions; it does not argue with you, but it fulfills your wishes. All things that have happened to you are based on thoughts impressed on the subconscious mind through belief. The subconscious mind will accept your beliefs and your convictions.

It is like the soil; it will accept any seed that you deposit in it, whether it is good or bad. Remember: Anything that you accept as true and believe in will be accepted by your subconscious mind, and brought into your life as a condition, experience, or event. Ideas are conveyed to the subconscious mind through feeling.

We will use an illustration: The conscious mind is like the navigator or man at the bridge of a ship. He directs the ship, and signals orders to the men in the engine-room which consists of all of the boilers, instruments, gages, etc. The men in the engine-room do not know where they are going; they follow orders. They would go on the rocks if the man on the bridge issued faulty or wrong instructions, based on his findings with the compass, sextant, or other instruments. The men in the engine-room obey him, because he is the director. They do not talk back to the captain; they simply carry out orders.

The captain is the master of the ship; his orders are followed out; likewise, your conscious mind is the captain, the master of your ship. Your body and all of your affairs represent the ship. Your subconscious mind takes the orders you give it based upon your belief and suggestions accepted as true.

Another simple illustration is this: When you repeatedly say to people, "I do not like mushrooms," then the time comes for you to be served mushrooms, you get indigestion, because your subconscious mind says to you, "The boss does not like mushrooms." This is an example probably amusing to you; nevertheless, this is an example of the relationship between the conscious and subconscious mind.

When a woman says, "I wake up at three o'clock if I drink coffee at night"; whenever she drinks it, the subconscious mind nudges her, as if to say, "The boss wants you to stay awake tonight."

The heart is called the subconscious mind in ancient allegories. The Egyptians knew that the heart was the subconscious mind, but they did not call it by that name.

The Chaldeans and the Babylonians called it by different names. You can impress your subconscious mind, and your subconscious mind will express what is impressed upon it. Any idea that is emotionalized or felt as true will be accepted by your subconscious mind.

If you want a healing, for example, get silent, relax, breathe easily, immobilize your attention, think of the healing power within your subconscious mind; affirm that the organ of your body is healing now. As you do that, there must be no resentment or bitterness in your heart; you must forgive everyone. You can repeat this healing process three or four times daily. Remember that your subconscious mind made the body, and can heal it also. People are constantly affirming the healing of an organ or a part of their body; then ten or fifteen minutes afterwards, they say, "Oh, I am getting worse; I'll never be healed. I am incurable." This mental attitude or these negative statements neutralize the previous, positive affirmation.

If a surgeon operated on you, cut out your appendix, and in the next few minutes ran back and opened you up again to see how you were getting along; then a half hour later ran back and opened you up again, he would probably kill you by poisoning. You kill or prevent your healing by using negative statements.

There is a subconscious mind within you; you should learn how to use it in the same manner as a man learns to use electricity. Man controls electricity with wires, tubes, and bulbs, plus his knowledge of the laws of conductivity and insulation, etc. We must learn about the tremendous power and the intelligence within us, and use it wisely.

Many men are beginning to realize the true importance of the subconscious mind. In business many men are using it to achieve success and promotion. Edison, Ford, Marconi, Einstein, and many others have used the subconscious mind;

it has given to them the insight and the "know how" for all of their great achievements in science, industry, and art. Research has shown that the ability to bring into action the subconscious powers has determined the success of all of the great scientific and research workers. There is a tremendous dynamo within you, and you can use it. You can also be completely released from tension and frustration. You can discover the abundant energy within you enabling you to energize and vitalize all parts of your body.

We are told, for example, that Elbert Hubbard declared that his most important ideas came while he was relaxed, or working in the garden, or going for a walk; the reason being when the conscious mind is relaxed, the subjective wisdom comes to the fore. There are oftentimes inspirational uprushes when the conscious mind is completely relaxed.

How often have you wondered at night what the answer to a particular problem was, and when you turned the request over to the subconscious mind, it gave you the solution in the morning. This is the meaning of the old adage, "Night brings counsel." If you want to wake up at seven o'clock in the morning, and you suggest seven o'clock to the subconscious mind, the subconscious mind will wake you at seven o'clock on the dot.

A mother may be nursing a sick child, and she falls asleep; but before she goes to sleep, she suggests to the subconscious mind that she will awaken if the child's temperature goes up, or when it needs medicine, or perhaps cries. There may be a thunderstorm going on while the mother sleeps; yet she is not awakened by the storm; however, when the child cries, she is immediately awakened. This is a simple function of the subconscious mind.

CHAPTER 2

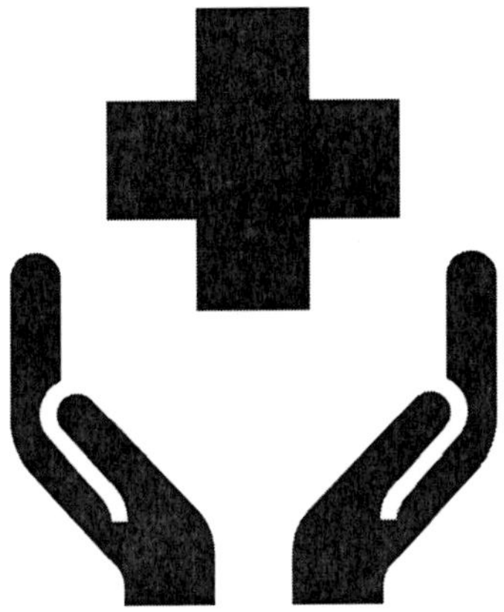

THE SUBCONSCIOUS MIND AND HEALTH

The subject of mental therapeutics is creating a widespread interest all over the world at the present time. Man is gradually awakening to the healing powers resident in his subconscious mind. It is a well-known fact that all of the various schools of healing effect cures of the most wonderful character. The answer to all of this is that there is one universal healing principle: namely, the subconscious mind, and one process of healing which is faith. This is why Paracelsus stated this great truth: "Whether the object of your faith be real or false, you will nevertheless obtain the same effects."

It is an established fact that cures have taken place in various shrines throughout the world, such as in Japan, India, Europe, and the American continent. You will find many widely differing theories, each presenting indubitable evidences of healing. Obviously to the thinker, there must be some underlying principle common to them all. Regardless of the geographical location, or the means used, there is only one healing principle, and the process of every healing is faith.

The first thing to remember is the dual nature of your mind. The subconscious mind is constantly amenable to the power of suggestion; furthermore the subconscious mind has complete control of the functions, conditions, and sensations of your body.

I venture to believe that all of the readers of this book are familiar with the fact that the symptoms of almost any disease can be induced in hypnotic subjects by suggestion.

For example, a subject in the hypnotic state can develop a high temperature, flushed face, or chills according to the nature of the suggestion given. By experiment you can suggest to the person that they are paralyzed and cannot walk; it will be so. Pain can also be induced in any part of the body. By illustration you can hold a cup of cold water under the nose of the hypnotic subject, and tell him, "This is full of pepper; smell it!" He will proceed to sneeze. What do you think caused him to sneeze, the water or the suggestion?

If a man says he is allergic to Timothy grass, you can place a synthetic flower or any empty glass in front of the nose of such a person in a hypnotic state, and tell him it is Timothy grass; he will portray the usual allergic symptoms. This indicates that the cause of the disease is in the mind; the healing of the disease can also take place mentally.

We realize that remarkable healings take place through osteopathy, chiropractics, medicine, and naturopathy, as well as through all of the various churches, but we maintain that all of these healings are brought about through the subconscious mind – the only healer there is.

Notice how it heals a cut on your face caused by shaving; it knows exactly how to do it. The doctor dresses the wound; he says, "Nature heals it." Nature refers to natural law, the law of the subconscious mind, or self-preservation, which is the function of the subconscious mind. The instinct of self-preservation is the first law of nature; your strongest instinct is the most potent of all auto-suggestions.

You have just learned that you can induce disease in your own body, or that of another through suggestion, in defiance of your natural instincts. It is perfectly natural and obvious that suggestions in harmony with instinctive auto-suggestion would have greater power.

It is easier to maintain and restore health, than it is to bring about sickness in the body. The faith that brings about healing is a certain mental attitude, a way of thinking, an inner certitude, an expectancy of the best.

In the healing of the body it is, of course, desirable to secure the concurrent faith of both the conscious and subconscious mind; however, it is not essential if the person will enter into a state of passivity and receptivity by relaxing the mind and the body, and getting into a sleepy state. I have known people who have completely denied matter and their bodies; yet they received marvelous healings. I have known others who said the world was real, that matter was real, and that their bodies were real; they, likewise, have had wonderful healings.

The point is that any method, technique, or process you may use which will bring about a change in the mind or a new mental atmosphere is legitimate; results will follow. Healing is due to a changed mental attitude, or to a transformation of the mind.

Paracelsus said, "Whether the object of your faith be true or false, you will nevertheless obtain the same effects." Thus if you believe in the bones of saints to heal, or if you believe in the healing power of certain waters, you will get results, because of the powerful suggestion given to your subconscious mind; it is the latter that does the healing. The witch doctor with his incantations heals by faith also.

Any method which causes you to move from fear and worry to faith and expectancy will heal. True, scientific, mental healing is brought about by the combined function of the conscious and subconscious mind scientifically directed.

The man who denies the ulcer on his hand, though he has one, who even denies his body, and who says all that is visible and tangible has no real existence may get a healing;

all of this would be absurd to you. The question arises, "How does the man get a healing when he protests against such statements claiming they insult his intelligence?" The reason is very obvious when you know how the subconscious mind works.

The man is asked to relax his mind and body, to get into a quiet, passive, receptive state; then the objective senses are partially suspended and in abeyance. He is in a sleepy state, and the subconscious mind is amenable to suggestion. The practitioner then suggests wonderful words of perfect health which enter his subconscious mind; the client finds immense relief and perhaps a complete healing. The practitioner is not handicapped by antagonistic auto-suggestions of the patient arising from objective doubt of the power of the healer or the correctness of the theory. In the sleepy, drowsy state of the conscious mind resistance is reduced to a minimum; hence results follow.

There are a great number who claim that because their theory produces results, it is, therefore, the correct one; this, as explained in this chapter, cannot be true. You know there are all types of healing. Mesmer and others healed by claiming they were sending forth a certain magnetic fluid. Other men came along and said all of this was nonsense, that the healing was due to suggestion.

All of these groups, such as psychiatrists, psychologists, osteopaths, chiropractors, physicians, and all churches are using the one universal, healing power resident in the subconscious mind. Each may proclaim the healings are due to their theory. The process of all healing is a definite, positive, mental attitude, an inner certitude, or a way of thinking called *faith*. Healing is due to a confident expectancy which acts as a powerful suggestion to the subconscious mind releasing its healing potency.

One man does not heal by a different power than another. It is true he may have his own theory and method. There is only one process of healing, and that is faith; there is only one healing power, namely, your subconscious mind. Select the theory and method which you prefer. You can rest assured, if you have the faith, you shall get results.

In the Los Angeles *Examiner* some time ago, John McDowell described tests being conducted in prayer therapy at Redlands University under the title, "Psychosomatic Tests Bare Prayer's Power." He writes as follows: "Dr. William R. Parker, 37-year-old director of the clinic, today revealed for the first time that early results of prayer therapy in a group of twenty arthritic, tubercular, ulcer, and speech impediment patients have been favorable.

"These patients, who agreed to practice prayer therapy in addition to the university clinic's regular group psychological therapy, have been making greater progress than the clinic's regular patients, Dr. Parker said.

"For example: A stomach ulcer patient, relying solely on prayer and group therapy, has reported that, for the last three weeks, all symptoms of his ailment have disappeared.

"A Redlands University professor, afflicted most of his life with a severe case of stuttering which years of various treatments failed to correct, today has no trace of speech impediment after six months of prayer therapy.

"Another teacher, forced into retirement a year ago because of tuberculosis, is now back at his teaching job, apparently cured.

" 'This man's doctor, – a tuberculosis specialist – recently gave him a sputum test,' Dr. Parker said. 'The test turned up negative, and the doctor was certain a mistake had been made. He immediately made another test, and that was negative, too.'

"Dr. Parker – a doctor of psychology, not medicine – stresses that prayer therapy is no 'quackish' miracle cure-all, but a scientific approach to prayer and its effect on the subconscious mind.

"The subconscious mind, in the eyes of the still-pioneering psychosomatic medicine world, is the fountainhead of many of mankind's afflictions, including arthritis, asthma, hay fever, multiple sclerosis, tuberculosis, ulcers, and high blood pressure.

"The psychosomatic theory – hotly disputed by the medical profession – is that such ailments start as functional disorders in the subconscious and develop into organic disease, which doctors treat by attacking the symptoms rather than the cause.

"Prayer therapy, according to Dr. Parker, is a psychosomatic attempt to attack the causes of these disorders in the subconscious.

" 'Four basic personality difficulties are at the root of everything that goes wrong in the subconscious mind,' Dr. Parker said. 'They are fear, hate, guilt, and inferiority.'

"In the Redlands prayer-therapy experiments, these basic difficulties are first ferreted out through a series of standard psychological tests given to patients participating in the project.

"Subsequently, the patients meet in a ninety-minute group session once a week to discuss their problems. At these meetings, each patient is given a sealed envelope containing information on one detrimental aspect of his or her personality uncovered in the tests.

"Once at home, the patients open the envelopes, learn a new, undesirable phase of their personality, and resolve that particular difficulty in prayer daily until the next group meeting.

"There is only one 'must.' Each patient is required to pray regularly each night before he or she retires.

" 'We insist on a prayer at that time, because the last thing that a person is thinking before going to sleep is most likely to penetrate to the subconscious,' Dr. Parker said.

"Dr. Parker, who first tried out his prayer theories on himself during an onset of ulcers three years ago, said most of the patients have to be taught how to pray.

"The clinic's prayer-therapy patients are taught a positive approach to prayer, stressing love, and an uplifting concept of God and the universe.

"Our prayers are not a begging for health, but are affirmations of the healing of the unhealthy element the patient wants to attack stated in such a positive, repetitious manner that eventually it sinks into the subconscious, and becomes a part of that person,' Dr. Parker said.

" 'In that manner, through prayer, destructive aspects within the subconscious can be attacked and eventually overcome, thus eliminating the basic causes of their physical ills.' "

In the Wilshire Ebell Theatre where I speak to an overflow audience each Sunday, we have a period called "the healing silence." The first thing I do is ask the audience to relax, let go, and to stop the wheels of their mind. The purpose is to quiet down the doubting Thomas (conscious mind), and insert a new idea such as health, peace, joy, and abundance into the receptive minds of the listeners. Those who are impregnated will give birth to a healing or an answer to their prayer. This is the kinetic action of the subconscious mind. Many report excellent results every Sunday as attested to by grateful letters.

I would like to stress a few important factors here relative to the workings of the subconscious mind. A man came to me one time and asked me why it was when he kept on saying to himself, "I have no headache," that the pain did not go away? The subconscious mind will not easily accept this contradiction; it accepts only what you believe and feel as true, or accept, as possible. If you mentally accept the possibility of the execution of your idea, the subconscious will cooperate. In order to impress the subconscious mind, you must gain its cooperation. If you can convince the subconscious mind you have no headache, the headache will go away.

I suggested to him this method: Declare: " It is passing away," over and over again quietly and peacefully. In this way he would be better able to sell the idea or conclusion to the wise, deep self, called the subconscious mind. He got results; he added something to it, "It will never return." For years he has never had any migraine attacks from which he suffered frequently. He had a belief or an expectancy that every Tuesday and Saturday morning, he would get migraine attacks. This feeling acted as an auto-suggestion to his subconscious mind; the latter obliged him by seeing to it that he would have a headache at the time specified. It simply said, "It is Tuesday morning; the boss wants a headache." The negative suggestion was removed by the above counter suggestion.

Here is another instance: A very brilliant woman came to me some years ago stating that she had psoriasis on her body which would go away by applying an ointment, but that as soon as the salve was discontinued, it would return. She was not resenting anyone; she was very religious, and seemingly well balanced emotionally. In talking to her I discovered that she lived in constant fear of its return. As a matter of fact this was a very powerful suggestion to her subconscious mind, since it is controlled by suggestion and belief; it responded accordingly.

She would affirm two or three times a day: 'I am whole, pure, and perfect; my skin is perfect; I am healed." Nothing happened. You can readily see what happened in her case. Every time she said, "My skin is perfect," it started a quarrel in her mind; something within her said, "No, your skin is not perfect!"

The following technique worked for her in a wonderful way. She started to say for five or ten minutes three or four times a day: "It is changing now for the better." This created no quarrel in her conscious or subconscious mind; results followed; it gradually disappeared, and it has never returned. I am sure she ceased suggesting its return. (What I fear most has come upon me.)

Trust the subconscious mind to heal you. It made your body, and it knows all of its processes and functions. It knows much more than your conscious mind about healing and restoring you to perfect balance. The subconscious mind, sometimes called the deep-self, knows more about your body than all of the wisest men in the world. Never try to coerce or force the mind. We do not infer that some people who say, "I am whole, pure, and perfect," do not get results; of course they do, because they succeed in convincing themselves of it. Blind belief and faith will bring results due to the subjective faith of the individual.

A psychologist friend of mine told me that one of his lungs was infected. X-rays and analysis showed the presence of tuberculosis. At night before going to sleep, he would quietly affirm, "Every cell, nerve, tissue, and muscle of my lungs are now being made whole, pure, and perfect. My whole body is now being restored to health and harmony." These are not his exact words, but they represent the essence of what he said. A complete healing followed in about a month's time; subsequent X-rays showed a perfect healing.

I wanted to know his method, so I asked him why he repeated the words prior to sleep. Here is his reply: "The kinetic action of the subconscious mind continues throughout your sleep-time period; hence give the subconscious mind something good to work on as you drop off into slumber." This was a very wise answer. In suggesting harmony and health, he never mentioned his trouble by name.

I strongly suggest that you cease talking about your ailments or giving them a name. The only sap from which they draw life is your attention and fear of them. Like the above mentioned psychologist become a good mental surgeon; then your troubles will be cut off like dead branches are pruned from a tree.

If you are constantly naming your aches and symptoms, by the law of your own mind these imaginings tend to take shape, greatly feared."

A technique of impressing the subconscious mind is as follows: This consists essentially in inducing the subconscious mind to take over your request as handed it by the conscious mind. This "passing over" is best accomplished in the reverie-like state. Know that in your deeper mind is infinite intelligence and infinite power. Just calmly think over what you want; see it coming into fuller fruition from this moment forward. Be like the little girl who had a very bad cough and sore throat. She declared firmly and repeatedly, "It is passing away now. It is passing away now." It passed away in about an hour. Use this technique with complete simplicity and naiveté.

In using the subconscious mind you infer no opponent; you use no will power. You use imagination, not will power. You imagine the end and the freedom state. You will find your intellect trying to get in the way, but persist in maintaining a simple, child-like, miracle-making faith. Picture yourself without the ailment or problem. Imagine the emotional accompaniments of the freedom-state you crave. Cut out all red tape from the process. The simple way is always the best.

Remember that your body possesses an organic mechanism reflecting the interplay of the conscious and subconscious mind; viz., the voluntary (cerebro-spinal nervous system) and the involuntary nervous system. These two systems may work separately or synchronously. The vagus nerve connects the two systems in the body. When you study the cellular system and the structure of the organs such as eyes, ears, heart, liver, bladder, etc., you learn they consist of groups of cells which possess a group-intelligence whereby they function together, and are able to take orders and carry them out in deductive fashion at the suggestion of the master mind (conscious mind). This is why the group intelligence of the lungs responded to the constructive, positive suggestions of the psychologists previously mentioned in this chapter.

In this book our purpose is to remove the mystery of the workings of the mind, in order to know better its *modus operandi.* In the relaxed state the subjective mind comes to the surface, and begins to work on the correct patterns suggested by the healer. The kinetic action of the mind comes into play by way of the vagus nerve. Between sleeping and the waking state the mind breaks through from its material thraldom and the limitations of time and space, and asserts its innate freedom.

Dr. Evans, a student of Quimby, was able to suspend the conscious mind, and by an interior illumination, attended with no loss of consciousness of external surroundings, was able to diagnose disease.

Clairvoyance is one of the powers of the subconscious mind which enabled Quimby, Dr. Evans, and many others to clearly see the internal structure of man, the nature and extent of the disease, plus the cause behind it; this proved a great aid in their healing of patients. The explanation of the mental and emotional cause of their ailments was the solution in most cases.

The usual procedure is as follows:

1. Take a look at the problem.
2. Then turn to the solution or way out known only to the subconscious mind.
3. Rest in a sense of deep conviction that it is done.

Do not weaken your treatment by saying, "I hope so!" or "It will be better!" The cellular set-up of your body will follow faithfully and honestly whatever blue print the conscious mind hands over to them via the subconscious, sometimes called subjective, or involuntary mind. Your feeling about the work to be done is "the boss." Know that health is yours! Harmony is yours! Become intelligent by becoming a vehicle for the infinite, healing power of the subconscious mind.

The reasons of failure are: Lack of confidence and too much effort. Suggest to the subconscious mind to the point of conviction; then relax. Get yourself off of your hands. Say to conditions and circumstances, "This, too, shall pass." Through relaxation you impress the subconscious mind enabling the kinetic energy behind the idea to take over, and bring it into concrete realization.

A careful study of the single-celled organism shows us what goes on in our complex body. Though the mono-cellular organism has no organs, it still gives evidence of mind-action and reaction performing the basic functions of movement, alimentation, assimilation, and elimination. Dr. Alexis Carrell's findings in heart experiments of chicks are significant, pointing to the basic finding that life functions despite the lack of complete, organistic equipment.

The body of man portrays the workings of his inner mind. Our real powers are resident in the subconscious mind. No one knows all of the workings of the subconscious mind; for it is infinite in its scope. We learn what we can about how it works; then we use it accordingly. People say there is an intelligence which will take care of the body if we let it alone. This is true, but the difficulty is that the conscious mind always interferes with its five-sense evidence based on outer appearances, leading to the sway of false beliefs, fears, and mere opinion. When fear, false beliefs, and negative patterns are made to register in the subconscious mind through psychological, emotional conditioning, there is no other course open to the subconscious mind except to act on the blue-print specification offered to it.

The subjective self within you works continuously for the general good, reflecting an innate principle of harmony behind all things. Study the works of Edison, Carver, Einstein, and many others who without too much outer education knew how to tap the subconscious mind for its manifold treasures. Have a reason for the faith in you. You cannot get very far if you do not believe in what you do not see. I do not see love, but I feel it; I do not see beauty, I see it manifested. Subjective faith is often greater in a puny body of a garret-loving poet than in the stronger frame of a prize fighter. Our greatest failing is a lack of confidence in the powers of the subconscious mind. Get acquainted with your inner powers.

Of what use is it to know in principle that you are perfect if you cannot bring it out? Self-realization, plus feeling, is the only key to healing. To get results is no proof your method is scientific or sound.

I knew a man who was told to wave a rabbit's foot around his head seven times, and a big wart would fall off. He believed it, and the result followed. The rabbit's foot had nothing to do with it; it was due to a law of mind. Mental acceptance and belief were the causes, and the disappearance of the wart was the effect. If you are tense and anxious, the subconscious mind will pay no attention to you in a tough situation.

A house-owner once remonstrated with a furnace-repair man for charging two hundred dollars for fixing the boiler. The mechanic said, "I charged five cents for the missing bolt, and one hundred and ninety-nine dollars and ninety-five cents for knowing what was wrong."

Similarly, your subconscious mind is the master mechanic, the all-wise one, who knows ways and means of healing any organ of your body, as well as your affairs.

Decree health, and the subconscious mind will establish it, but relaxation is the key. “Easy does it.” Do not be concerned with details and means, but know the end result. Get the *feel* of the happy solution of your problem, whether it is health, financial, or employment, etc. Remember how you felt after you had recovered from a severe state of illness. Bear in mind that the feeling is the touchstone of all subconscious demonstration. Your new idea must be felt subjectively in a finished state – not in the future – but as *now* coming about.

One of our students who attended our lectures on The Miracles of The Mind had severe eye trouble which the doctor said necessitated operation. He was instructed how to use the Nancy School technique: Take a little phrase or affirmation, easily graven on the memory, and repeat it over and over again like a lullaby.

Each night this man, as he went to sleep, entered into the drowsy, meditative state, the state akin to sleep. His attention was immobilized and focused on his eye doctor. He imagined the doctor was in front of him, and he plainly heard, or imagined he heard, the doctor saying to him, “A miracle has happened!” He heard this over and over again every night for perhaps five minutes or so before going to sleep. At the end of three weeks he went to the ophthalmologist who had previously examined his eyes, and he said, to this client, “This is a miracle!” What happened? He impressed his subconscious mind, using the doctor as an instrument or a means of convincing or conveying the idea. Through repetition, faith, and expectancy he impregnated the subconscious mind. The subconscious mind made the eyes; within it was the perfect pattern, and immediately it proceeded to heal the eyes. This is another example of The Miracles of Your Mind.

CHAPTER 3

THE SUBCONSCIOUS MIND AND ALCOHOLISM

The alcoholic is mentally ill, and he needs a mental overhauling. The problem drinker, the compulsive drinker, or the habitual drinker does not drink normally. The problem drinker is the chronic alcoholic; he drinks for days, weeks, and even months at a time. The alcoholic says that a passion seizes him periodically to drink. He is a victim of a habit, because the acts leading to intoxication have been repeated so often, he has established a subjective pattern in his subconscious mind.

Because the alcoholic has already yielded to his craving, he fears that he will yield once more; this contributes to his repeated falls due to the suggestions given to his subconscious mind. It is his imagination which causes the alcoholic to return to drinking intermittently. The images which have been impressed on his subconscious mind begin to bear fruit. He imagines a drinking bout in which glasses are filled and drained; then he imagines the following sense of ease and enjoyment, a feeling of relaxation. If he lets his imagination run wild, he will go to the bar or buy a bottle.

The drinker uses effort and will power to overcome the habit, or "cause," as he calls it. The more effort or will power he uses, the more hopelessly engulfed does he become in the quicksand.

Effort is invariably self-defeated, eventuating always in the opposite of what is desired. The reason for this is obvious: The suggestion of powerlessness to overcome the habit dominates his mind; the subconscious mind is always controlled by the dominant idea. The subconscious mind will accept the strongest of two contradictory propositions. The effortless way is the best.

The first drink starts the alcoholic off. This is due to a subconscious tendency or urge established through habit.

There is a Law of Reversed Effort which was explained by the French school of therapeutics in 1910. It means this: When your desire and your imagination are in conflict, the imagination invariably gains the day. For example, you will hear an alcoholic say, "I took a lot of pains, I tried so hard, I forced myself, I used all the will power I had," etc. He has to be made to realize that herein lies his error; then he begins to conquer the habit.

If, for example, you were asked to walk a plank on the floor, you would do so without question. Now suppose the same plank were placed twenty feet up in the air between two walls, would you walk it? Your desire to walk it would be counteracted by your imagination – your fear of falling. The dominant idea would conquer. Your desire, will, or effort to walk would be reversed, and the dominant idea of failure would be reinforced.

If a man says, "I want to give up alcohol, but I cannot" he may wish to give it up, but the harder he tries, the less he is able. Never try to compel the subconscious mind to accept your idea by exercising will power. Such attempts are doomed to failure. The subconscious mind accepts the dominant of two contradictory statements. It is like the man who is poverty stricken saying, "I am wealthy." In most instances his statement makes him poorer. The simple reason for this is that his belief in poverty is much greater than his belief in abundance, so he is suggesting more lack to himself each time he makes the statement. This illustrates the Law of Reversed Effort. In other words, the opposite result from that which was intended follows.

In using the subconscious to heal alcoholism you must engage its cooperation. The subconscious mind will accept your feeling, your belief, or your conviction. The alcoholic avoids the conflict which arises in his mind by using the sleeping technique. By entering into a sleepy, drowsy state, effort is reduced to a minimum. The conscious mind is submerged to a great extent when in a sleepy state. The best time to impregnate the subconscious mind, as the French school pointed out in 1910, is prior to sleep. The reason for this is that the highest degree of outcropping of the subconscious occurs just prior to sleep and just after we awaken. In this state the negative thoughts which tend to neutralize your desire and so prevent acceptance by the subconscious no longer present themselves.

Here is a simple method a chronic alcoholic for forty years used. I wrote this out for him:

Assume a comfortable posture, relax your body, and be still. Get into a sleepy state and in that sleepy state say quietly, over and over again as a lullaby, "I am completely free from this habit; sobriety and peace of mind reign supreme." Repeat the above slowly, quietly, and lovingly for five or ten minutes night and morning. At the end of three weeks he lost all desire to drink. Each time he repeated the above statement its emotional value became greater. When the urge came, he repeated the above formula out loud to himself. By this means he induced the subconscious to accept his idea and a healing followed.

I remember treating an alcoholic in Rochester, New York, some years ago. He said to me, "I had not had a drop in six months, and I was congratulating myself. All my friends were patting me on the back telling me what wonderful will power I had."

"Then," he added, "an uncontrollable urge seized me, and I have been drunk for two weeks."

This had happened time and again with this man. The effort of his will suppressed his desire temporarily, but his continued effort to suppress made matters worse. His repeated failures convinced him that he was hopeless and powerless in controlling his urge or obsession. This idea of being powerless operated, of course, as a powerful suggestion to his subconscious, increased his impotence, and made his life a wreck.

I taught him how to harmonize the function of the conscious and subconscious mind. When the two cooperate, the idea or desire is realized.

His reasoning mind admitted that if he had been conditioned negatively he could be conditioned positively. His mind entertained the idea that he could succeed. He ceased thinking of the fact that he was powerless to overcome the habit. Moreover, he understood clearly that there was no obstacle to his healing other than his own thought. Therefore, there is no occasion for great mental effort or mental coercion. To use force is to pre-suppose that there is opposition. When the mind is concentrated on the means to overcome a problem, it is no longer concerned with the obstacle.

This man made a practice of relaxing his body, getting into a sleepy, drowsy, meditative state; then filling his mind with the picture of the desired end, knowing the subconscious would bring it about in the easiest way. He imagined his daughter congratulating him on his freedom, saying to him, "Daddy, it's wonderful to have you home."

He had lost his family through drink. He was not allowed to visit them; his wife would not speak to him.

Regularly, systematically, he used to sit down and meditate in the way outlined. When his attention wandered, he brought it back to the picture of his daughter with her smile, tonal qualities, and the scene of his own home.

All this was a reconditioning of his mind. It was a gradual process. He kept it up; he persevered knowing that sooner or later he would succeed in impregnating his subconscious with the mental picture. I told him the conscious mind was the camera, and his subconscious was the sensitive plate on which he registered and impressed the picture. This made a profound impression on him; his whole aim was to impress the picture and develop it in his mind. Your film is developed in the dark; likewise, your mental picture is developed in the darkhouse of the subconscious mind.

Realizing his conscious mind was the camera, he used no effort; there was no mental struggle. He quietly adjusted his thought, and focused all his attention on the scene before him. He became absorbed in its reality, somewhat like a sponge absorbing water. It's a sort of mental absorption whereby you are completely identified with the picture. Sometimes you are so engrossed or absorbed in reading a newspaper article, you can't hear a loved one speak to you.

He got into this mental atmosphere, repeated it frequently, and knew a healing would follow. When the temptation to drink came, he knew it was his imagination taking him back to the drinking bout, so he would switch off that scene, cut the film, so to speak, and see his daughter, feel her embrace, and hear her voice. The secret of his success was that he confidently expected to experience the picture he was developing in his mind.

You are a ship, and thought is your helm. Change the direction of the helm (your thought); as a result you change the direction of your ship.

Get acquainted now with that infinite reservoir of strength and healing power within you which is the subconscious mind. If you are an alcoholic, admit it; do not dodge the issue. Many people remain alcoholics, because they refuse to admit it.

Your disease is an instability, an inner fear. You are refusing to face life, and so you try to escape your responsibilities through the bottle. The interesting thing about an alcoholic is that he has no free will; he thinks he has; he boasts about his will power. The habitual drunkard says bravely, "I will not touch it anymore," but he has no power to back it up, because he does not know where to locate it.

The alcoholic is living in a psychological prison of his own making, and is bound by his beliefs, opinions, training, and environmental influences. He is like most people; i.e., he is a creature of habit. He is conditioned to react the way he does.

The alcoholic must build the idea of freedom and peace into his mentality, so that it reaches his subconscious mind. The latter being all-powerful will free him from all desire for alcohol; then the alcoholic who has the new understanding of how his mind works can truly back up his statements, and prove it to himself.

Your subconscious mind is conditioned by your beliefs and habits. If the alcoholic has a keen desire to free himself from the habit, he is fifty-one percent healed already. When he has a greater desire to give it up than to continue it, he will not experience too much difficulty in gaining complete freedom.

The alcoholic must recondition his mind. There are ways and means of doing this. When you think good, good follows; when you think evil, evil follows; these are simple examples of laws of mind. If a man dwells and broods on sorrow, he meets sorrow and gloom in his outer experience. If he dwells on peace and good fortune in his business, it will prosper. To know the possibilities of such laws of mind is to be seized with a new inspiration and a new faith.

The alcoholic learns that whatever thought he anchors his mind upon, the latter magnifies. If the alcoholic engages his mind on the concept of freedom (freedom from the habit) and peace of mind, and if he keeps focused on this new direction of his attention, he generates feelings and emotions which gradually emotionalize the concept of freedom and peace. Whatever idea is emotionalized is accepted by the subconscious mind, and brought to pass.

The alcoholic must realize that something good can come out of his suffering; he has not suffered in vain. However what good is it to continue to suffer?

To continue as an alcoholic is only to bring about mental and physical deterioration and decay. Begin to say, "No!" to the urge now. Realize that the power in your subconscious mind is backing you up. Even though you may be seized with melancholia and the shakes, begin to imagine the joy and freedom that is in store for you; this is the law of substitution. Your imagination took and peace of mind. You will suffer a little bit, you to the bottle; let it take you now to freedom but it is for a constructive purpose; you will bear it like the mother in the pangs of childbirth, and you will, likewise, bring forth a child of the mind. Your subconscious mind will give birth to sobriety.

Your thinking controls you, whether you know it or not. You are now fully aware of the fact that your subconscious mind accepts without question the thoughts you impress upon it. You can now begin to control your life. *To discipline your mind* means to think constructively and harmoniously.

One time I read an article about Goethe. He was wont to hold imaginary, mental conversations with friends. For example, he would get still and quiet and imagine one of his friends answering him in the way he wanted, with characteristic gestures and tone of voice. He solved many of his problems that way. So can you.

Many have asked me about their reason or cause for drinking to excess. There are, of course, many reasons. It may be that a man is resenting his wife, or his job, or his employer. Maybe he is jealous, or he has an inferiority or rejection complex. I have discovered in treating alcoholics that there is nearly always a deep sense of guilt.

I am now thinking of a married man, with four children, supporting and secretly living with another woman during his business trips. He was ill, nervous, irritable, cantankerous, and could not sleep without drugs. He had pains in numerous organs of his body which doctors could not diagnose. He was a confirmed alcoholic when I saw him. The reason for his periodic sprees was a deep unconscious sense of guilt. He had violated the ancient code and this troubled him. The religious creed he was brought up on was deeply lodged in his subconscious mind; he drank excessively to heal the wound of guilt.

Some take morphine and codeine for severe pains, he was taking alcohol for the pain or wound of the mind. It is the old story of adding fuel to the fire.

He listened to the explanation of how his mind worked, he faced his problem, looked at it, and gave up his dual role. He knew that his drinking was an unconscious attempt to escape. The hidden cause lodged in the subconscious had to be eradicated; then the healing followed.

When he began to look at his problem in the light of reason, it was dissipated. He began to use this treatment three or four times a day. "My mind is full of peace, poise, balance, and equilibrium. The Infinite Power lies stretched in smiling repose within me. I am not afraid of anything in the past, the present, or the future. Infinite Intelligence leads, guides, and directs me in all ways. I now meet every situation with faith, poise, calmness, and confidence. I am now completely free from the habit; my mind is full of inner peace, freedom, and joy. I forgive myself; then I am forgiven. Peace, Sobriety, and Confidence reign Supreme in my mind."

He repeated this frequently knowing what he was doing, and why he was doing it. Knowing what he was doing gave him the necessary faith and confidence. I explained to him that as he said these statements out loud, slowly, lovingly, and meaningfully, they would gradually sink down into his subconscious; like seeds they would grow after their kind.

I explained to him that his subconscious mind was like a garden; by planting lovely seeds he would reap a wonderful harvest. It is the nature of an apple seed to bring forth an apple tree. These truths which he concentrated on went in through his eyes; his ears heard the sound; the healing vibration of these words reached his subconscious mind, and obliterated all the negative mental patterns which caused all the trouble. Light dispels darkness; the positive thought destroys the negative. He became a transformed man within a month.

Of course, as you know, people will give you all manner of excuses or alibis as to why they drink. They may blame their drinking on some tragedy in the home, some crisis in their life, lack of money, or education. The real reason is negative thinking which has brought about an emotional maladjustment. "As a man thinketh in his heart, so is he." The word *heart* is an ancient word meaning the subconscious mind. In simple language it is saying, "As you think and feel, so are you in all departments of your life."

Emerson said, "A man is what he thinks all day long." This is the answer and the whole story. The cause is in yourself, in your habitual thinking, your mental attitude, and reaction to life. The alcoholic addict is really seeking to escape some sense of bondage or some subconscious restriction. In other words the alcoholic lacks confidence and poise.

I told a woman one time not to give any more money to her son as he spent it all on drink. I said, "You are only contributing to his delinquency."

"Oh," she said, "he kneels down, kisses the Bible, and swears he will never touch another drop. I believe him; then I give him the money. He seems so penitent, remorseful, and so full of condemnation of himself for the way he acted, that I think he means it."

I explained to her that these were idle statements on the part of her son and really meant nothing; under no circumstances should she give him any more money. I spent some time with her explaining that the boy had no free will, but was just boasting about his will power to give up drinking. His statements and oaths that he would never touch it anymore were meaningless, as he had no power to back them up. In other words, he did not know where the power was, nor how to locate it.

She brought him to see me. He came rather reluctantly making the usual statement that he was not an alcoholic. I told him to stop this nonsense; admit it openly, and not dodge it. That is the first step in healing. Many remain alcoholics, because they refuse to admit they are.

This boy was condemning himself saying, "I suppose I'm no good." Alcohol took him into a world of temporary illusion where in his morbid imagination he was king for a day. This gave him a false sense of confidence and a temporary sense of self-sufficiency. He admitted that if he took one drink, he lost all control, and drank until he fell unconscious. The reason for this is obvious: His mental control was rendered null and void due to a subconscious pattern engraved on his mind over a long period of time. It is like a track on which the train moves. He had established a mental track in his mind on which ran images of drinking bouts, of glasses filled, images associated with feeling of enjoyment and success.

The minute this confirmed drunkard took a drink that was a suggestion for another and another until he fell unconscious. He had subjectified a belief in the necessity of alcohol; the law of the subconscious being that of compulsion, the moment he took one he was compelled to take another. This young man said what all alcoholics say, "If I don't take the first drink I'm all right, but the minute I take the first, I lose control."

The reason is that the one drink brings on an outcropping of the subconscious mind which, in the case of the alcoholic, due to long habit and conditioning says to him, "Have another! Have another!" His subconscious belief and fear is his governor, and controls his conduct and actions.

Man is bound by his beliefs, opinions, training, and environmental influences. He is conditioned to react the way he does. Life is forever seeking to express itself through man. The desire for true place, peace of mind, abundance, and security are cosmic urges within all men. There is a law of mind which, when understood, enables man to realize his cherished desires. The cause of all confusion, strife, and problems in the world is man's failure to realize his heart's desires. Show man the powers of his own subconscious mind; tell him that if he will imagine the end; feel it subjectively, and remain faithful to his ideal, the subconscious will bring it to pass. People who try and stifle desire have really an unconscious impulse toward self-destruction or self-oblivion. When man begins to believe in a Power greater than himself lodged in his own unconscious depths, he is on the way to health, happiness, and peace of mind.

There is nothing new about the following technique. It is as old as man. The most ancient wisdom available said, "As a man imagines and feels, so is he."

- *The first step*: Get still; quiet the wheels of the mind. Enter into a sleepy, drowsy state. In this relaxed, peaceful, receptive state you are preparing for the second step.

- *The second step*: Take a brief phrase which can readily be graven on the memory, and repeat it over and over again as a lullaby. (Nancy School technique). Use the phrase, "Sobriety and peace of mind are mine now, and I give thanks." To prevent the mind from wandering repeat it aloud or sketch its pronunciation with lips and tongue as you say it mentally. This helps its entry into the sub-conscious mind. Do this for five minutes or more. You will find a deep emotional response from the subconscious. It is wonderful.
- *The third step*; Just before going to sleep, practise what Goethe used to do. Imagine a friend, a loved one in front of you. Your eyes are closed; you are relaxed and at peace. The loved one is subjectively present and is saying to you, "Congratulations!" You see the smile; you hear the voice. You touch the hand and the face; it's all so real and vivid. The word *congratulations* implies complete freedom. Hear it, over and over again, until you get the reaction which satisfies.

The above technique is sound, psychological procedure, and is an excellent means of conveying an idea to the subconscious mind. You know you will go where your vision is. The wishful thinker is a man who does not believe in the possibility of the execution of his idea or desires. He is the day dreamer. The scientific thinker imagines the end – the victory. He sees fulfillment and accomplishment, and maintains his faith every step of the way knowing that having imagined and felt the end, he has willed the means to the realization of the end.

When fear knocks at your door, when doubt, worry, and anxiety cross your mind, behold your vision. Trust it, believe in it, and an Almighty Power will be generated by your subconscious giving you full confidence and strength. Keep on keeping on "until the day breaks and the shadows flee away."

CHAPTER 4

THE SUBCONSCIOUS MIND AND WEALTH

The trouble with most people is that they have no invisible means of support when business falls away, or the stock market drops, or they lose their investments; they seem helpless. The reason for such insecurity is that they do not know how to tap the subconscious mind. They are unacquainted with the inexhaustible storehouse within.

A man with a poverty-type mind finds himself in poverty-stricken conditions. Another man with a mind filled with ideas of wealth is surrounded with everything he needs. It was never intended that man should lead a life of indigence. You can be wealthy, have everything you need, and plenty to spare. Your words have power to cleanse your mind of wrong ideas, and to instill right ideas in their place.

I have talked to many people during the past thirty-five years; their usual complaint is, "I have said for weeks and months that I am wealthy; I am prosperous, and nothing has happened." I discovered that when they said, "I am prosperous; I am wealthy," they felt within that they were lying to themselves.

One man told me, "I have affirmed until I am tired that I am prosperous. Things are now worse. I knew when I made the statement, that it was obviously not true." His statements and those of the others were rejected by the conscious mind, and the very opposite of what they affirmed and claimed was made manifest.

Auto-suggestion succeeds best when it is specific, and it does not produce a mental conflict or argument; hence the statements made by this man made matters worse, because they suggested his lack. The subconscious accepts only your convictions and beliefs, not just words or statements. The dominant idea or belief is always accepted by the subconscious mind.

The following is a way to overcome this conflict for those who have this difficulty. Make this practical statement frequently, particularly prior to sleep: "By day and by night I am being prospered in all of my interests." This will not arouse any argument, because it does not contradict the subconscious mind's impression of financial lack.

I suggested to one business man whose sales were very low, and he was greatly worried, that he sit down in his office, get quiet, and repeat this statement over and over again: "My sales are improving every day. I am advancing, progressing, and getting wealthier every day." This statement engaged the cooperation of the conscious and subconscious mind; results followed.

The above is a very simple, unique way of impressing the subconscious mind with the idea of wealth. Perhaps you are saying as you read this chapter, "I need wealth and success." This is what you do: Repeat for about five minutes to yourself three or four times a day, "Wealth–Success." These words have tremendous power. They represent the inner power of the subconscious mind. Anchor your mind on this substantial power within you; then conditions and circumstances corresponding to their nature and quality will manifest in your life. You are not saying, "I am a success," or "I am wealthy." You are dwelling on real powers within you. There is no conflict in the mind when you say, "Wealth," or "Success"; furthermore, the feeling of wealth and success will well up within you, as you dwell upon these ideas.

The feeling of wealth produces wealth; the feeling of being successful produces success; keep this in mind at all times. The subconscious mind is like a bank – a sort of universal bank; it magnifies whatever you deposit or impress upon it, whether it is good or evil.

You sign blank checks when you make such statements as: "There is not enough to go around;" or "There is a shortage;" maybe, "I will lose the mortgage;" etc. If you are full of fear about the future, you are also writing a blank check, and attracting negative conditions to you. The subconscious mind takes your fear and belief as your requests, proceeding in its own way to bring obstacles, delays, lack, and limitation into your life. To him that hath the feeling of wealth, more wealth shall be added; to him that hath the feeling of lack, more lack shall be added. The subconscious mind gives you compound interest also. Every morning as you awaken deposit thoughts of prosperity, success, wealth, and peace; dwell upon these concepts; busy your mind with them as often as possible. These positive thoughts will find their way as deposits in your subconscious mind, and bring forth abundance and prosperity.

I can hear you saying, "Oh, I did that and nothing happened." You did not get results, because you indulged in fear thoughts perhaps ten minutes later, and neutralized the good you had affirmed. When you place a seed in the ground, you do not dig it up.

Suppose, for example, you are going to say, "I shall not be able to make that payment!" Before you get further than, "I shall – " stop the sentence, and dwell on a positive, constructive statement, such as, "By day and by night I am being prospered in all my ways."

To prosper means to advance along all lines in wisdom, understanding, and material possessions. Money represents wealth; it is a symbol of exchange; it represents freedom, opulence, luxury, and refinement. I do not know of anyone who says that he has too much; in all probability he is looking for more.

Most people are under the impression that the value of their money is dependent on so much gold in South Africa or in the vaults of the United States Treasury; others live in fear that the currency will be devaluated, and that they will lose. When the blood is circulating perfectly and harmoniously in your body, the physician says that you are healthy; like-wise, when money is circulating freely in your life, meeting all of your needs, and there is always a surplus, you are prosperous.

For example, if you listen to the radio, and you hear that there is a crash in the stock market, resulting in a worried or frightened feeling, you are conditioned and affected by some set of statistics or by a news broadcast. Your financial security and wealth are dependent upon your subjective or inner feeling of prosperity.

When you are seeking to convey the idea of wealth and success to your subconscious mind, be sure you never make foolish statements, such as: "I despise money." "It is an evil thing." "It is the root of all evil." Such an attitude of mind will cause money to take wings and fly away from you. You would then be giving two conflicting orders to the subconscious mind; one would neutralize the other, and nothing would happen.

Money has taken many forms down through the ages. What you really want is to have a subconscious conviction that money will always be in constant circulation in your life, meeting all of your needs at every moment of time and every point of space.

Money is essential for your economic health in this country; therefore, you should have all you need and a surplus. Begin now to believe and claim that money is wonderful. Begin to love money and be friendly with it; you will always have plenty; you will never want.

Love is an emotional attachment. Except you love your work, or profession, you cannot be a true success. Love always magnifies and multiplies. Love the, idea of wealth until it becomes embodied subjectively. Write this down in big letters in your mind: What you love, you increase. What you criticize, fades out of your life.

You are familiar with this fundamental fact: When money is circulated freely in a country, its financial condition is healthy. Let there be a healthy circulation of money in your life also, particularly in your mental attitude. Believe that money is good; think of all of the good you can do with it. Become a mental inlet and outlet for a constant stream of wealth forever flowing to you and forever flowing from you in a perfect circulation.

If you are having financial difficulties, trying to make ends meet, it means you have not convinced your subconscious mind that you will always have plenty and some to spare. You know men and women who work a few hours a week, and make fabulous sums of money. They do not strive or slave hard. Do not believe the story that the only way you can become wealthy or successful is by the sweat of your brow and hard labor. It is not so; the effortless way of life is the best. Do the thing you love to do, and do it for the joy and thrill of it. Sing at your work; you will, if you love it; also, if you love your work, you are bound to be a success.

An executive I know receives a salary of $60,000 yearly. Last year he was on a ten month cruise, seeing the world and its beauty spots. He has convinced his subconscious mind that he is worth that much money. He told me that many men in his organization getting less than one hundred dollars per week knew more about the business than he did, and could manage it better, but they had no ambition and no ideas.

Money is simply a subconscious conviction on the part of the individual. You will not become a millionaire by saying, "I am a millionaire. I am a millionaire." You will grow into a wealth-consciousness by building into your mentality the ideas of wealth and success.

One of our students who was formerly a seventy-five dollar a week salesman is now a sales manager at a salary of twelve thousand yearly. It all happened within a period of a month.

Every morning as this person shaved, he would look into the mirror, and say to himself, "You are wealthy; you are a big success;" this went on for weeks. In about eight weeks he was suddenly promoted over the heads of eighty other salesmen. While shaving, you are relaxed. As previously outlined, you can convey an idea to the subconscious mind by repeating it again and again at intervals with faith and a joyous expectancy.

Here is a question frequently asked in our large and enthusiastic classes held at the Wilshire Ebell Theatre: "If I need a certain amount, such as, one thousand dollars, should I just concentrate on that?" You could do that, and it would work. However, the general and best procedure is not to think of money in terms of any particular or set sum. Think of it in terms of plenty to sustain you with ease and perfect freedom of action. The reason for this is that whatever you impress on the subconscious mind is always increased and multiplied like the grains of wheat sown in the ground bring forth of its kind a hundredfold.

The subconscious mind works under a law of abundance. Nature is lavish, extravagant, and bountiful. Increase your estimate of yourself. If you bargain with life for a penny a day, the universe will respond accordingly. Many people have a keen desire for more money, but they have a subconscious pattern of seventy-five dollars a week; therefore, that is what they demonstrate; whereas they could demonstrate much more.

Here is a simple technique for you to increase your consciousness of wealth; use these statements several times a day: "I like money; I love it; I use it wisely, constructively, and judiciously. Money is constantly circulating in my life. I release it with joy, and it returns to me multiplied in a wonderful way. It is good and very good." This will help you get the right attitude toward money.

Never criticize money by saying, "It is filthy lucre; it is bad; it is tainted." You cannot attract what you criticize. When you begin to think things through, you will realize that real wealth depends on the circulation of wonderful ideas in your mind which well up from the subconscious levels.

A young detective desiring more money, used the above mentioned formula. One morning he awakened with an intense desire to write a short story based on one of his experiences. He sat down; ideas came freely; his story was accepted; then he wrote many others, and was paid handsomely for these articles. Wealth came to him as ideas in his own mind. Your mind, also, can reveal to you a new invention, the material for a new book, or play. Make use of your subconscious mind.

One sales manager I knew used to get ideas for his promotional sales campaign when he awakened in the morning. He became the president of the company; they never had a sales manager like him.

Your subconscious mind is never short of ideas; there are within it an infinite number of ideas ready to flow into your conscious mind, and appear as cash in your pocket book in countless ways. This process will continue to go on in your mind regardless of whether the market goes up or down, or whether the pound sterling or dollar drops in value. Your wealth is never truly dependent on bonds, stocks, or money in a bank; these are really all symbols necessary and useful, of course. The point I wish to emphasize is that if you convince your subconscious mind that wealth is yours, and that plenty of money is always circulating in your life, you will always have it regardless of the form it takes.

If you believe that wealth or money is dependent on your job or more hours of work, you have a limited concept; you are bound by your own beliefs. This is a world of cause and effect. If you worry and fret about money, this mood of lack will produce a greater lack of money. Your mental attitude is the cause; less money is the effect.

There is one emotion which is the cause of financial lack in the lives of many. Most people learn this fact the hard way. It is envy. For example, if you see a competitor depositing large sums of money in the bank, and you have only a meagre amount to deposit, does it make you envious? The way to overcome this emotion is to say to yourself, "Isn't it wonderful! I rejoice in that man's prosperity. I wish for him greater and greater wealth."

Do you know what you are doing? You are actually impressing the subconscious mind with the idea of wealth! To entertain envious thoughts is devastating, because it places you in a very negative position; therefore, wealth flows from you, instead of to you. If you are ever annoyed or irritated by the prosperity or great wealth of another, claim immediately that you truly wish for him greater prosperity in every possible way. This will neutralize the negative thoughts in your mind, and cause a greater measure of wealth to flow to you by the law of your own subconscious mind.

Maybe you know someone who is always trying to make ends meet; they seem to have a great struggle with money. Have you listened to their conversation? In many instances their conversation runs along this vein: They are constantly condemning those who have succeeded in life, and who have put their heads above the crowd. Perhaps they are saying, "Oh, that fellow has a racket; he is ruthless; he is a crook." This is why they lack; they are condemning the thing they desire and want. The reason they speak critically of their prosperous associates is because they are envious and covetous of the other's prosperity. The quickest way to cause wealth to take wings and fly away is to criticize and condemn others who have more money than you.

Do you say you never had a chance? Are you blaming your relatives, your mother, or father, because they never aided you financially. Stop doing it immediately. Learn that the secret to wealth is the correct use of your own mind. All of the resources of that infinite mind are behind you seeking expression through you, if you will only have a receptive, mental attitude.

If you are worried and critical about someone whom you claim is making money dishonestly, cease worrying about him. You know such a person is using the law of mind negatively; the law of mind takes care of him. Be sure not to criticize him, for the reasons before assigned.

If you are experiencing a financial block, the obstruction is in your own mind. You can now destroy that mental block. Get on mental, good terms with everyone.

As you go to sleep tonight, practice the many techniques which we occasionally refer to. Repeat the word, "Wealth," quietly, easily, and feelingly. Do this over and over again as a lullaby. Lull yourself to sleep with the one word, "Wealth." You should be amazed at the results. Wealth should flow to you in avalanches of abundance; this is another example of The Miracles of The Subconscious Mind.

CHAPTER 5

HOW TO APPLY THE SUBCONSCIOUS MIND TO MARITAL PROBLEMS

The best time to prevent a divorce is before marriage. Ignorance of the powers within you is the cause of all of your marital trouble. Learn how to attract the right wife or husband. For instance, if you are a girl seeking a husband, do not begin to tell yourself all of the reasons why you cannot get married; rather tell yourself all of the reasons why you *can* be happily married. Eradicate the word *cannot* from your vocabulary. He can, who believes he can!

You are now acquainted with the way the subconscious mind works. You know that whatever you impress upon it, shall be experienced in your world. Begin now to impress your subconscious mind with the qualities and characteristics you admire in a man.

This is one technique: Sit down at night in your armchair; close your eyes; let go; relax the body; become very quiet, passive, and receptive. Talk to your subconscious mind, and say to it, "I am now attracting a man into my experience who is honest, sincere, loyal, kind, faithful, and prosperous. He is peaceful and happy. These qualities are sinking down into my subconscious mind now. As I dwell upon these qualities, they become a part of me. I know there is an irresistible law of attraction, and that I attract to me a man according to my subconscious belief. I attract that which I feel as true in my subconscious mind. In other words I know that according to the law, I will attract a man in accordance with my feelings, beliefs, and impressions made on my subconscious mind regarding the type of man I seek."

Practice this process of impregnating your subconscious mind; then you will have the joy of attracting a man having the qualities and characteristics you mentally dwelt upon. The subconscious intelligence will open up a pathway whereby both of you will meet according to the irresistible and changeless law of your own subconscious mind. Have a keen desire to give the best that is in you of love, devotion, and cooperation. Be receptive to this gift of love which you have given to your subconscious mind.

Marriage between man and woman should be an act of love. Honesty, sincerity, kindness, and integrity are forms of love. Each should be perfectly honest and sincere with the other. There is not a true marriage when the man marries a woman for her money, social position, or to lift his ego, because there is no sincerity or honesty there. The marriage is not of the heart. When a woman says, "I am tired working; I want to get married, because I want security;" her premise is false; she is not using the laws of mind correctly. Her security depends upon her knowledge of the interaction of the conscious and subconscious mind and its application.

For example, a woman will never lack for wealth or health if she applies the technique outlined in the respective chapters of this book. Her wealth can come to her independent of her husband, father, or anyone else. A woman is not dependent on her husband for health, peace, joy, inspiration, guidance, love, wealth, security, happiness, or anything in the world. Her security and peace of mind come from her knowledge of the inner powers within her, and her constant use of the laws of her own mind in a constructive fashion. Marrying for money or to get even with someone is, of course, a farce and a masquerade.

A man and a woman must be subjectively united in the sense that a real love or sense of oneness prevails; in other words two hearts are united in love, freedom, and respect.

A number of people have said to me, "Oh, we love each other, why should we bother getting married?" The answer to this is extraordinarily simple: What we subconsciously feel and accept as true is always objectified or made manifest on the screen of space. Their reasoning, therefore, is false and insincere. The law of mind is, "As within, so without."

Let us take the case of a man or a woman who has made an honest mistake. She now finds herself married to a drug-addict; he refuses to work; she has to support him; he is ruthless and cruel. It is true that due to her state of mind, she attracted that man; yet she is not condemned to live in a world of misery brought about by her own mood or ignorance. Had she used her subconscious mind in the right way, this would not have happened. (I am sure that if you fell into the gutter, slipped perhaps on a banana peel, it would be silly to condemn yourself and stay in the gutter. The obvious thing to do would be to get up out of the gutter, wash yourself, and keep on going.) The woman herein referred to, packed her belongings, and left this man. She realized it was an intolerable situation. Surely this woman is not condemned to live with this man when their hearts and minds are miles apart. You can tie two people together with a rope; yet they can be as far apart as the poles in thought, feeling, and perspective.

You are divorced mentally when your mind and heart are else-where. To stay together in such circumstances is chaotic from all angles. Marriage is a union of two hearts; there is no marriage where the hearts are not bound together in love and peace. Adultery takes place in the heart first. The heart is the seat of the emotions. If you are resentful, hateful, and critical of your partner, you have already committed adultery in your heart.

To direct your mental and emotional operations along destructive and negative channels is to commit adultery. Always remember the adulterous state takes place in the mind. Bodily acts follow mental states; they do not precede.

Perhaps as you read these pages, you are saying, "I know a young couple who got married recently. They both used the laws of mind; they seemed perfectly happy in every way. Now they are contemplating a divorce." The mental attitude which attracted and endeared them to each other must be maintained and strengthened, in order to preserve the marriage. If a disagreement arises or some slight argument occurs, and one of the partners engages the mind on a negative idea such as resentment or hostility, he is uniting with the error in his mind, and it is destructive to marital happiness.

The little arguments and quarrels which married people engage in will not hurt; it is the sustained grudge or ill feeling which does the damage. When the harsh words said are all forgotten and forgiven a few minutes later, no harm has been done. It is when the feeling of being hurt is prolonged, that the danger lies.

If a man begins to brood, grows morbid against his wife, because of the things she said or did, he is committing adultery, since he is mentally engaged in bitterness. This mood will endanger the marriage except he forgives and radiates love and goodwill to his partner. Let the man who is bitter and resentful swallow his sharp remarks; let him go to great length to be considerate, kind, and courteous. He can deftly skirt the differences. Through practice and mental effort, he can get out of the habit of antagonism; then he will be able to get along better not only with his wife, but with business associates also. Assume the harmonious state, and eventually you will find peace and harmony.

Let us have a few remarks about the nagging wife. Many times the reason she is a nagger is because she gets no attention; oftentimes it is a craving for love and affection. Give it to her. There is also the nagging type of woman who wants to make the man conform to her particular pattern. This is about the quickest way in the world to get rid of a man.

The wife and the husband must cease being scavengers – always looking at the petty faults or errors in each other. Let each give attention and praise to the positive and wonderful qualities in the other.

A great mistake is to discuss your marital problems or difficulties with neighbors and relatives. Suppose, for example, a wife says to the neighbor, "John never gives me any money; he treats my mother abominably; drinks to excess, and he is constantly abusive and insulting." Now this wife is degrading and belittling her husband in the eyes of all of the neighbors and relatives; he no longer appears as the ideal husband to them. Never discuss your marital problems with anyone except a trained counselor. Why have many people thinking negatively of your marriage? Moreover, as you discuss and dwell upon these shortcomings of your husband, you are actually creating these states within yourself. Who is thinking and feeling it? You are! As you think and feel, so are you.

Relatives will usually always give you the wrong advice; it is usually biased and prejudiced, because it is not given in an impersonal way. Any advice you receive which violates the golden rule – which is a cosmic law – is not good or sound. It is well to remember that no two human beings ever lived beneath the same roof without clashes of temperament, periods of hurts, and strain. Never display the unhappy side of your marriage to your friends. Keep your quarrels to yourself. Refrain from criticism and condemnation of your partner.

If there are children in the home, let the father praise their mother; let him call attention at times to her fine qualities and the happy aspects of the home.

A husband must not try and make his wife over into a second edition of himself. The tactless attempt to change her in many ways is so foreign to her nature; these attempts are always foolish; many times they result in a dissolution of the marriage. These attempts to alter her destroy her pride and self-esteem, and arouse a spirit of contrariness and resentment that proves fatal to the marriage bond.

Adjustments are needed, of course, but if you have a good look inside of your own mind, and study your character and behaviour, you will find so many shortcomings there to keep you busy the rest of your life. If you say, "I will make him over into what I want," you are looking for trouble and the divorce court. You are asking for misery. You will have to learn the hard way that there is no one to change but yourself.

If you have a marital problem, ask yourself what it is you want; then realize that you can achieve that goal. You would solve your marital problem in the same way as any other problem. Define clearly what you want; then realize that what the mind engages in, it creates.

A woman told me one time that after thirty years her husband began to drink heavily, neglecting his home and children. She began to claim peace and harmony in her home and heart. She paid no attention to the circumstances or conditions. She quietly engaged her mind on her goal, knowing that her subconscious mind would bring about and magnify what she gave her attention to. Harmony and peace were again restored after a few months devotion to her true goal. This is an illustration of The Miracles of The Subconscious Mind.

By resenting and fighting the situation, this woman would only make matters worse. If there is quarreling and bickering in the home, turn your attention away from personalities, environments, and conditions, and focus your attention on your ideal, which is love, peace, and harmony. As you feed your mind upon these ideas, the subconscious mind will respond and bring about harmony.

I am often asked this question, "If one of the partners has an intense desire to terminate the marriage, and the other has an equally intense desire to remain united in marriage, and they are both sincere, what will happen?" In such cases there is a mental tug of war; this is a house divided against itself; sooner or later it will dissolve; however, their attitude of mind may prolong the situation.

The proper and correct way to solve this marital problem is to lift the thought above personalities and conditions, and begin to direct your thought to your true desire, trusting the infinite intelligence within you to bring about the perfect solution. Through the right application of the law of your subconscious mind, you can bring harmony where discord is, and resurrect peace where confusion reigns; moreover, the right application of your subconscious mind can dissolve a bad marriage.

Do not let foolish pride, anger, and a desire to get even take you to the divorce court, when all of the while your heart is one with the husband you left. Let love, goodwill, and kindness lead you back to the one you love in your heart. You can heal any problem through the right application and direction of your subconscious mind. Listening to the intuition or guidance which comes from the subjective wisdom within you would have perhaps prevented you from contracting the present marriage. You did not know how to use it; now you do. If you had a bad start, you can adjust it now by using the procedure and techniques outlined in this chapter. By exalting, and lifting up your partner in thought and feeling, and always cherishing the lovely qualities which brought you together, you can make your marriage a beautiful experience and a joy forever.

CHAPTER 6

THE SUBCONSCIOUS MIND AND GUIDANCE

In explaining the workings of the subconscious mind to our recent college class, one of the men present said that the answer to his problem came to him while he was shaving. The reason for this was that while he was shaving, he was relaxed; then the wisdom and intuition of the subconscious mind came to the surface mind.

This man had been giving intense, conscious application to his problem for several days. By adhering to the following instructions he got results: As he was about to go to sleep at night, he would say, "I am now turning this request over to my deeper mind; I know it has the answer, and I will receive it."

In the first chapter we told you that the subconscious mind will awaken you at six in the morning, because you are thinking about six o'clock in the morning before you go to sleep. In the same manner the subconscious mind took up his case; having the superior wisdom, it logically deduces the perfect answer, and gave it to him.

You will often note that immediately after awakening, the answer will come to you, because you are still half asleep and half awake; there is an outcropping of the wisdom of the subconscious mind at that time.

When you are beset with a problem, what do you do? Many people will worry and fret about the problem; this makes matters worse, because the subconscious mind always magnifies what we impress upon it.

Many liken the subconscious mind to a bank; you are constantly making deposits in this universal bank. Be sure you deposit seeds of peace, harmony, faith, and goodwill; these will be magnified a thousand fold; then prosperity and good fortune will be your harvest. How do you find yourself reacting to the problems of the day and to your environment? If you react with anger, bitterness, criticism, and resentment, you are making these deposits in the bank within you. When you need strength, faith, and confidence, you cannot draw them out, because you have not placed these qualities in your bank.

Begin now to deposit joy, love, peace, and good humor; busy your mind with these things; then the subconscious bank will give you compound interest. It will magnify exceedingly beyond your wildest dreams.

When you have what you term a difficult decision to make, or when you fail to see the solution to your problem, begin at once to think constructively about it. If you are fearful and worried, you are not really thinking. Real thought consists in contemplating whatsoever things are true, just, honest, lovely, and of good report. True thinking is free from fear. The real reason why you are fearful is because you have a false concept, or you are taking a wrong view of things. Probably you believe that external things, conditions, and circumstances control you, and that they are causative. Remember you have dominion over your environment and conditions.

Here is a simple technique which you can follow: Quiet the mind; still the body; tell the body to relax; it has to obey you. It has no volition, initiative, or intelligence of itself; it is an emotional disc which records your beliefs and impressions. Immobilize your attention; focus your thought on the solution to your problem. Try and solve it with your conscious mind. Think how happy you would be about the perfect solution. If your mind wanders, bring it back gently. In this sleepy, drowsy state, say quietly and positively, "The answer is mine now; I know my subconscious mind knows the answer." Live now in the mood or feeling of the solution. Sense the feeling you would have if the perfect answer were yours now. Let your mind play with this mood in a relaxed way; then drop off to sleep. You may fall asleep sooner than you expected, but you were thinking about the answer; the time was not wasted. When you awaken, and you do not have the answer, get busy about something else. Probably when you are preoccupied with something else the answer will come into your mind, like toast pops out of the toaster.

Never think about your problem in this manner: "Things are getting worse. I will never get the answer." "I see no way out." "It is hopeless." You are reversing the law, and undoing the good work you have done. Thinking about the answer activates the intelligence of the subconscious which knows all, sees all, and has the "know how" of accomplishment.

The subconscious mind has the power to create; it also obeys the orders given to it by the conscious mind. Remember always this simple truth: The conscious mind has the power of choice; the subconscious does what it is told to do. The latter accepts your beliefs and convictions, and brings them into your experience. It is an infinite, creative power.

Sometime ago I received a clipping from a magazine describing how Dr. Banting solved his problem of diabetes. He had made a profound study of the disease. One night he was awakened in the early hours of the morning with the answer to extract the substance from the degenerated, pancreatic duct of dogs; this was the origin of insulin, which has helped millions of people.

It does not follow that you will always get an answer overnight; the answer may not come for weeks or months. Do not be discouraged. Keep on turning it over every night to the subconscious mind prior to sleep, as if you had never done it before. One of the reasons for the delay may be that you look upon it as a major problem. You may believe it will take a long time to solve it.

The subconscious mind is timeless and spaceless. Go to sleep believing you have the answer now, and that the solution is yours now. Do not postulate the answer in the future. Have an abiding faith in the outcome. Become convinced now, as you read this book, that there is an answer, and a perfect solution for you.

Here is a very simple technique used from time immemorial to get an answer from the subconscious mind: Calmly think over what you want, such as, the answer, the harmonious solution, or the right decision. The best time to turn over a request is just before going to sleep. Relax the body; still the wheels of your mind; suggest sleep to yourself. You will begin to feel sleepy, but you are still consciously aware and capable of directing your attention.

For example, you can hear a baby cry next door, or you can hear someone walking around the house. You are in a state akin to sleep, between the waking and sleeping state. (The Nancy School of Therapeutics calls this state *the reverie.*) In this drowsy, meditative state you induce the subconscious mind to take over your problem or request; this *passing over* to the subconscious mind is best accomplished through the above process. You infer no opponent; you use no will power. You imagine the end, the solution, and the freedom state. Do this with complete naiveté and simplicity. Have a simple, childlike, miracle-making faith. Picture yourself without the problem. Cut out all of the red tape from the process.

The simple way is the best. This is an illustration: I lost a valuable ring; it was an heirloom; I looked everywhere for it, and could not locate it. I decided to practice what I preach! At night I talked to the subconscious in the same manner that I would talk to anyone. I said to it prior to dropping off to sleep: "You know all things; you know where that ring is, and you now reveal to me where it is." In the morning I awoke suddenly with the words ringing in my ear, "Ask Robert!"

I thought it very strange that I should ask Robert; however, I followed the inner voice of intuition.

Robert said, "Oh, yes, I picked it up on the sidewalk in front of the house. It is in my drawer; it did not seem very valuable, so I did not say anything about it!" The subconscious mind will always answer you if you trust it.

A young man in our recent class had this experience: His father passed on to the next dimension, and apparently left no will. However this man's sister told him that their father had confided to her that a will had been executed which was fair to all. All attempts to locate the will failed. During the closed class on The Miracles of The Subconscious Mind this young man put into practice what he heard. As he went to sleep, he said, "I now turn this request over to the subconscious mind; it knows just where that will is; it reveals it to me"; then he condensed his request clown to one word, "Answer," repeating it over and over again as a lullaby. He lulled himself to sleep with the word, "Answer."

This student had a dream that night, a very vivid, realistic dream, wherein he saw the name of a certain bank in Los Angeles and its address. He went there; found a safe deposit vault registered in the name of his father which solved all of his problems.

Your thought as you go to sleep arouses the powerful latency which is within you. For example, let us suppose you are wondering whether to sell your home, buy a certain stock, sever partnership, move to New York or stay in Los Angeles, dissolve the present contract or take a new one. Do this: Sit quietly in your arm chair or at the desk in your office; remember that there is a universal law of action and reaction. The action is your thought. The reaction is the response from your subconscious mind. The subconscious mind is reactive and reflexive; this is its nature. It rebounds, rewards, repays; it is the law of correspondence. It responds by corresponding. As you contemplate right action, you will automatically experience a reaction or response in yourself. You have now used the infinite intelligence resident in the subconscious mind to the point where it begins to use you; from then on your course of action is directed and controlled by the subjective wisdom within you, which is all wise and omnipotent. Your decision will be right; there will only be right action, because you are under a subjective compulsion to do the right thing. I use the word *compulsion*, because the law of the subconscious is compulsive.

Our subconscious convictions and beliefs dictate and control all of our conscious actions. The secret of guidance or right action is to mentally devote yourself to the right answer, until you find its response in you. The response is a feeling, an inner awareness, an overpowering hunch whereby you know that you know. You have used the power to the point where it begins to use you. You cannot possibly fail or make one false step while operating under the direction of the subjective wisdom within you.

Think of a garden; then you will understand the two-fold aspect of mind, and the subjective law by which it operates. The conscious mind plants the seed in the soil. It decides what kind of seed shall be planted. As you know the soil will grow whatever is planted, whether it is grapes or thorns.

Similarly, look upon the subconscious mind as the soil; it contains all of the elements necessary and essential for growth. Again let us realize it is the nature of the soil to *bring forth*, but as you know, it is not the slightest bit interested in what it brings forth. It does not care whether it brings forth a pear tree or an apple tree. All of the laws of nature would be violated should the soil refuse to produce or grow poisonous plants.

Exactly the same thing is true of the subconscious mind; it is a doer; it never questions or talks back to you. It accepts what you deposit in it, and produces it in your experience whether it is good or bad. Learn to use your subconscious mind constructively, wisely, and judiciously.

I want to stress this important fact: You will always receive guidance in respect to the subject in which you think about the most. The subconscious mind is impersonal and no respecter of persons. If, by illustration, you begin to think about how you can set fire to a certain building without being detected, ideas and thoughts will come to you for the evil and destructive uses of fire. The universal energy or power in and of itself is perfectly harmless; however, you can use it for constructive or destructive purposes.

Let us take the atomic energy about which we read so much; it is perfectly harmless. You know very well it is in the mind of man that the danger of atomic energy lies. He can use the atomic energy to warm or light a house or destroy thousands of people.

You receive guidance in accordance with what you habitually think about. If you think and dwell upon fears, troubles, and failure, you will be guided in the wrong direction, and more chaos and confusion will be experienced by you.

Take this great thought, and dwell upon it: There is nothing to fear in all of the universe! You have the power of control through the wise use of your subconscious mind. Sit down quietly now, and think of a beautiful lake on top of a mountain; it is a still, quiet night. On the surface of the quiet, placid lake you see mirrored the stars, the moon, and perhaps the trees nearby. If the lake is disturbed, you will not see the stars or the moon. Similarly quiet your mind, relax, and let go. Think of peace and stillness; then over the mirrored waters of your mind will move the answer to your question!

CHAPTER 7

OVERCOMING FEAR THROUGH THE SUBCONSCIOUS MIND

Emerson said, "Do the thing you fear, and the death of fear is certain." There was a time when the writer of this chapter was filled with unutterable fear when standing before an audience. The way I overcame it was to stand before the audience; do the thing I was afraid to do, and the death of fear was certain. When you affirm positively that you are going to master your fears, and come to a definite decision in your conscious mind that you are going to overcome, you release the power of the subconscious which flows in response to the nature of your thought.

One of our students told me that he was invited to speak at a banquet. He said he was panic stricken at the thought of speaking before a thousand people. He overcame the fear this way: For several nights he sat down in an armchair for about five minutes and said to himself slowly, quietly, and positively, "I am going to master this fear. I am overcoming it now. I speak with poise and confidence. I am relaxed and at ease." He operated a definite law of mind and overcame his fear.

The subconscious mind is amenable to suggestion and controlled by suggestion. When you still your mind and relax, the thoughts of your conscious mind sink down into the subconscious through a process similar to osmosis, whereby fluids separated by a porous membrane intermingle. As these positive seeds or thoughts sink into the subconscious area, they grow after their kind, and you become poised, serene, and calm.

A young lady was invited to an audition. She had been looking forward to the interview. However, on three previous occasions she failed miserably due to stage fright.

Here is the very simple technique which I gave her. Remember this young lady had a very good voice, but she was certain when the time came for her to sing that she would be seized with stage-fright. The subconscious mind takes your fears as a request, proceeds to manifest them, and bring them into your experience. On three previous auditions she sang wrong notes and finally broke down. The cause, as previously outlined, was an involuntary auto-suggestion; i.e., a silent fear thought emotionalized and subjectified.

She overcame it by the following technique. Three times a day she isolated herself in a room. She sat down comfortably in an armchair, relaxed her body, and closed her eyes. She stilled the mind and body as best she could. Physical inertia favors mental passivity, and renders the mind more receptive to suggestion. She counteracted the fear suggestion by its converse, saying to herself, "I sing beautifully, I am poised, serene, confident, and calm." She repeated this statement slowly, quietly, and with feeling from five to ten times at each sitting. She had three such "sittings" every day and one immediately prior to sleep. At the end of a week she was completely poised and confident, and gave a remarkable, wonderful audition. Carry out the above procedure with assurance and conviction, and the death of fear is certain.

Occasionally young men from the local university come to see me, and also school teachers, who seem to suffer from suggestive amnesia at examinations. The complaint is always the same – "I know the answers after the examination is over, but I can't remember the answers during the examination."

The idea which realizes itself is the one to which we invariably give concentrated attention. I find that each one is obsessed with the idea of failure. Fear is behind the temporary amnesia, and is the cause of the whole experience.

One young medical student was the most brilliant in his class; yet he found himself failing to answer simple questions at the time of written or oral examinations. I explained to him that the reason was he had been worrying and fearful for several days previous to the examination, these constant negative thoughts became charged with fear. Thoughts enveloped in the powerful emotion of fear are realized in the subconscious. In other words, this young man was requesting his subconscious mind to see to it that he failed, and that is exactly what it did. On the day of the examination he found himself stricken with what is called in psychological circles "suggestive amnesia.

A French psychologist named Baudouin said, "What we have to work for in overcoming fear is education of the imagination."

Here is how the young man overcame his fear. He learned that his subconscious mind was the storehouse of memory, and had a perfect record of all he had heard and read during his medical training. Moreover, he learned that the subconscious mind was responsive and reciprocal; the way to be en-rapport with it was to be relaxed, peaceful, and confident.

Every night and morning he began to imagine his mother congratulating him on his wonderful record. He would hold an imaginary letter from her in his hand and read congratulatory words. He would also feel the letter in his hand. As he began to contemplate the happy result, he called forth a corresponding or reciprocal response or reaction in himself. The all-wise and omnipotent power of the subconscious took over, dictated, and directed his conscious mind accordingly. He imagined the end. When he imagined and felt the end, he willed the means to the realization of the end. Following this procedure he had no trouble passing subsequent examinations. In other words the subjective wisdom took over compelling him to give an excellent account of himself. The law of the subconscious mind is compulsion.

There are many people who are afraid to go in an elevator, climb mountains, or even swim in the water. It may well be that the individual had unpleasant experiences in the water in his youth, such as having been thrown forcibly into the water without being able to swim.

I had an experience when I was about ten years of age. I fell accidentally into a pool and went down three times. I can still remember the dark water engulfing my head, and my gasping for air until another boy pulled me out at the last moment. This experience sank into my subconscious mind; for years I feared the water.

An elderly psychologist said to me, "Go down to the swimming pool, look at the water, and say out loud in strong tones, 'I am going to master you, I can dominate you;' then go into the water, take lessons, and overcome it." This I did. I learned that when you do the thing you are afraid to do, fear disappears.

It was only a shadow in my mind. When I assumed a new attitude of mind, the omnipotent power of the subconscious responded giving me strength, faith, and confidence, enabling me to overcome. I used the subconscious mind to the point where it began to use me.

Following is a process and technique for overcoming fear which I teach from the platform – it works like a charm.

Try it! Suppose you are afraid of the water, or a mountain, an interview, an audition, or you fear closed places. If afraid of swimming, begin now to sit still for five or ten minutes, for three or four times a day, and imagine you are swimming. Actually you are swimming in your mind; it is a subjective experience. Mentally you have projected yourself into the water. You feel the chill of the water and the movement of your arms and legs. It is all real, vivid, and a joyous activity of the mind. It is not idle day dreaming, for you know what you are subjectively experiencing in your imagination will be developed in your subconscious mind; then you will be compelled to express the image and likeness of the picture you impressed on your deeper mind; this is the law of the subconscious.

As you continue to discipline your mind this way, you are mentally immersed in the water and happy in it, consequently the fear passes; you will enter the water physically. I might say you will be compelled to give a good performance. You have consciously called upon the wonderful power of your subconscious which is all wise and powerful; this power controls you and governs you according to the nature of your call or request. This is a wonderful thing to know and a marvelous thing to do.

The president of a large organization told me that when he was a salesman, he used to walk around the block five or six times before he called on a customer. The sales manager came along one day, and said to him, "Don't be afraid of the boogie man behind the door, there is no boogie man; it's a false belief.

The manager told him that whenever he looked at his own fears, he stared them in the face and stood up to them, looking them straight in the eye; then they faded and shrank into insignificance.

Go out now and face that thing you are afraid of. If you are afraid to take that position, take it. Say to yourself "I can accomplish; I will succeed!" You will find a corresponding emotion or feeling generated by your subconscious. You will induce the mood or feeling of confidence, faith in yourself, and the joy of accomplishment. Fear is a thought in your mind, but confidence is a far more powerful thought; it fills your mind with a positive, constructive feeling and drives fear out.

A chaplain told me of one of his experiences in the second World War. He had to parachute from a damaged plane and land in a jungle. He said he was frightened, but he knew there were two kinds of fear, normal and abnormal. Normal fear is good; it is the law of self preservation. It is the subconscious mind telling you something must be done. It is sort of an alarm system that tells you to get out of the way of an oncoming car.

The chaplain said, "I began to talk to myself saying, 'John, you can't surrender to your fear; your fear is a desire for safety or security, for a way out.' "

He said that he knew there was a subjective intelligence which led the birds to their food and told them where to go in summer and winter. He began to claim, "Infinite Intelligence which guides the planets in their course is now leading and guiding me out of this jungle."

He kept saying this out loud to himself for ten minutes or more. "Then," he added, "something began to stir inside me, a mood of confidence began to seize me, and I began to walk. After a few days I came out miraculously, and was picked up by a rescue plane."

His changed mental attitude saved him. His confidence and trust in the subjective wisdom and power within him was the solution to his problem. He said, "Had I begun to bemoan my fate and indulge my fears, I would have succumbed to the monster *fear*, and probably have died of fear and starvation."

Whenever fear comes, go to the opposite immediately in your mind. To indulge in fear thoughts constantly and to engage your mind constantly with negative thoughts result in abnormal fear, obsessions, and complexes. To engage the mind with all the difficulties of your problem will only instill more fear until it assumes a size of catastrophic proportions. Finally there comes a sense of panic and terror weakening and sickening you. You can overcome fear of this nature when you know that the power of your subconscious can always change the objective conditions. Go within, claim, and feel your good – the solution. Know there is an Infinite Intelligence which responds and reacts to your thought and feeling.

Imagine the end; feel the thrill of victory. What you subjectively feel and imagine as true is the inner evidence of what will take place objectively. Your subconscious can free you. When fear thoughts come, contemplate the solution, the happy ending. Never fight negative or fearful thoughts. Always turn on the lamp of love, peace, and confidence within you. Most of our fears are imaginary.

The general manager of an organization told me that for three years he feared he would lose his position. He was always imagining failure. The thing he feared did not exist, save as a morbid, anxious thought in his own mind. His vivid imagination dramatized the loss of his job until he became nervous and neurotic. Finally he lost his position; he was asked to resign.

Actually he dismissed himself. His constant, negative imagery and fear suggestions to his subconscious mind caused the latter to respond and react accordingly. It made him make mistakes and foolish decisions which resulted in his failure as a general manager. The thing this man feared did not exist. His dismissal would never have happened had he immediately moved to the opposite in his mind.

No thought or concept, constructive or negative, can ever manifest except we emotionalize such concepts. The thoughts, concepts, and ideas have to penetrate the subconscious before they can affect us for good or evil.

If you look back in your life, you will agree with the writer that most of your fears, worries, and anxieties never came to pass. The reason for this was that you did not retain them long enough; likewise you did not charge them with a deep emotion. The general secret of banishing fear is to constantly fill your mind with constructive and positive thoughts. Fill the mind with thoughts of love, peace, and harmony. Give attention to your goal, ideal, the positives, the things you wish to experience in life. As you do this, an inner invisible movement of your subconscious will take place changing your world into the likeness of your inner imagery and contemplation.

During a recent round the world lecture tour, I had a two hour conversation with a prominent government official. He had a deep sense of inner peace and serenity. He said that all the abuse he receives politically from newspapers and the opposition party never disturbs him. His practice is to sit still for fifteen minutes in the morning and realize that in the center of himself is a deep, still ocean of peace. Meditating in this way, he generates tremendous power which overcomes all manner of difficulties and fear.

Some months ago, a colleague called him at midnight and told him that a group were plotting against him. This is what he said to his colleague: "I am going to sleep now in perfect peace. You can discuss it with me at ten A.M. tomorrow."

Notice how calm he was, how cool, how peaceful! He didn't start getting excited, tearing his hair, or wringing his hands. At his center he found the still water, an inner peace, and there was a great calm.

Your mind is composed of two areas, the conscious mind where we reason, and the great unconscious or subconscious depths which somewhat resemble the ocean into which many forgotten fears and false beliefs are lodged.

I met a man who came to my hotel in New Delhi, India, for consultation. He was from the British Isles. He had acute sinusitis, a deep sense of grief, and was haunted by unknown fears. I found in talking to him that he hated his father for many years, because the father had bequeathed all his estate to his brother. This hatred developed a deep sense of guilt in his subconscious mind; because of this guilt he had a deep, hidden fear of being punished; this complex expressed itself as migraine and sinusitis in his body.

Fear means pain. Love and good will mean peace and health. The fear and guilt which this man had were expressed as disease, or lack of ease or peace. The mucous membranes of his nose were always inflamed.

This young man realized that his whole trouble was caused by his own sense of guilt, self-condemnation, and hatred. His father had long since passed on to a higher dimension of life. Actually he was poisoning himself through hatred; he began to forgive himself. *To forgive* is to give something for. He practiced saying, "I completely forgive my father. He did what he believed right according to his light. I release him. I wish him peace, harmony, and joy. I am sincere, I mean it."

Then he cried for a long time. That was good. He lanced the psychic wound, and all the psychic pus came forth. His sinusitis disappeared. I have had a letter from him saying that the migraine attacks have ceased altogether. The fear of punishment which was lurking in his subconscious mind has now disappeared.

Use this perfect formula for casting out fear. "I sought the Lord, and He heard me, and delivered me from all my fears." The *Lord* is an ancient word meaning your subconscious mind.

Learn the powers of your subconscious, how it works and functions. Master the techniques given you in this chapter. Put them into practice now – today! Your subconscious will respond, and you will be free of all fears.

"I sought the Lord, and He heard me, and delivered me from all my fears."

INSPIRING QUOTES OF DR. JOSEPH MURPHY

Miracle working power of your subconscious mind can heal you of your sickness, making you vital and strong again.

Within your subconscious depths lie infinite wisdom, infinite power, and an infinite supply of all that is necessary.

You can bring into your life more power, more wealth, more health, more happiness, and more joy by learning to contact and release the hidden power of your subconscious mind.

Your subconscious mind is constantly amenable to the power of suggestion.

It is your right to discover this inner world of thought, feeling, and power, of light, love, and beauty.

Do the thing you are afraid to do, and the death of fear is certain. Say to yourself and mean it, "I am going to master this fear," and you will.

There is only one process of healing and that is faith. There is only one healing power, namely, your subconscious mind

You can build radiant health, success and happiness by the thoughts you think in the hidden studio of your mind.

The law of the subconscious mind works for good and bad ideas alike. This law, when applied in a negative way, is the cause of failure, frustration, and unhappiness. However, when your habitual thinking is harmonious and constructive, you experience perfect health, success, and prosperity.

Guidance is given you while you are asleep, sometimes in a dream. The headling currents are also released and in the morning you feel refreshed and rejuvenated.

Patience, kindness, love, good will, joy, happiness, wisdom and understanding are qualities which never grow old. Cultivate them and express them and remain young in mind and body.

The infinite intelligence within your subconscious mind can reveal to you everything you need to know at every moment of time and point of space provided you are open-minded and receptive.

Your subconscious mind is constantly amenable to the power of suggestion.

There is no true success without peace of mind.

All you have to do is unite, mentally and emotionally with the good you wish to embody. The creative powers of your subconscious will respond accordingly.

Radiate love, peace and good will to each other. These vibrations are picked up by the subconscious mind resulting in mutual trust, affection and respect.

Happiness is the harvest of a quiet mind. Anchor your thoughts on peace, poise, security and divine guidance and your mind will be productive of happiness.

If you imagine an objective clearly, you will be provided with the necessities through the wonder-working power of your subconscious mind.

A successful man is not selfish. His main desire in life is to serve humanity.

Once the subconscious mind accepts an idea, it begins to execute it.

All things that have happened to you are based on thoughts impressed on the subconscious mind through belief.

When you open your eyes in the morning say to yourself, I choose happiness today, I choose success today. I choose peace today.

You cannot be hurt by criticism when you know that you are master of your thoughts, reactions and emotions. This gives you the opportunity to pray and bless the other, thereby blessing yourself.

Remember that the subconscious mind has determined the success and wonderful achievements of all great scientific workers.

BIOGRAPHY OF
DR. JOSEPH MURPHY

Murphy, Joseph (20 May 1898-16 Dec. 1981), religious leader and writer, was born Joseph Denis Murphy in County Cork, Ireland, the son of Denis Murphy, the head of a Jesuit boys school called the National School of Ireland, and Ellen Connolly. Denis Murphy was one of the few laymen to teach in a church school in Ireland and was a deacon in the Roman Catholic Church. Joseph grew up in a devout religious home, attending his father's school and preparing to study for the priesthood, but he began to have doubts about church doctrine in his late teens and withdrew from the seminary. At around this time he experienced the healing of a malignancy, a recovery that he attributed to personal prayer, and this proved a turning point in his spiritual life.

Determined to explore new ideas, he moved to the United States in 1922, arriving at Ellis Island in New York with five dollars in his pocket and a limited command of English, since Gaelic had been the language of his family and schooling. He began working with other Irish immigrants as a day laborer, and when a fellow resident of his rooming house found him a job in a pharmacy he began taking courses leading to certification as a pharmacist. Within a few years he purchased the drugstore in the Algonquin Hotel, where he worked. When the United States entered World War I, he closed his successful business to join the army and served as a pharmacist in the medical unit of the 88th Infantry Division until 1918.

Murphy had been interested in religion since the medical recovery he associated with prayer, and while in the army he began to read about various faiths. When he returned to civilian life he abandoned pharmacology for travel and study, making trips to Europe and Asia to investigate other spiritual systems. In New York he began attending services at the Church of the Healing Christ, a part of the Church of Divine Science, one of the major denominations of the growing spiritual movement known as New Thought. An important influence on his thinking at this time was Thomas Troward (1847-1916), a British author whose books on spiritual metaphysics had a profound effect on the New Thought movement. Troward's involvement with Freemasonry led Murphy to become active in the order, in whose ranks he was to reach the 32nd degree. In the mid-1940s Murphy moved to Los Angeles, where he met Ernest Shurtleff Holmes (1887-1960), the founder of Religious Science, another branch of New Thought. This pioneer self-help writer, the author of the hugely successful book Creative Mind and Success (1919), guided Murphy to a full-time study of Religious Science and in 1946 he was ordained a minister of that denomination and began teaching at its Institute of Religious Science.

He later met Erwin Gregg, the president of the Association of Divine Science and, drawn back to that faith, he was reordained to its ministry in 1949. He became the director of the Church of Divine Science in Los Angeles; soon it had the largest congregation of any of that denomination's churches in the United States, with lectures attended by 1,300 to 1,500 people every Sunday. He also broadcast a weekly radio program to an audience said to exceed a million listeners. His sermons, lectures, and radio broadcasts were so popular that he summarized them in church bulletins and, to reach a larger audience, began to record and sell cassette tapes of them. Later his lectures were transcribed and sold in pamphlets for $1.50 to $3 at his church. In time these booklets, with their positive message of optimism and hope, were combined, edited, updated, and published in large editions. Sometime during the 1950s he married. There were no children born of this marriage, and his wife's name is not reported. During that decade he returned to school, earning a Ph.D. in psychology from the University of Southern California.

Described by one of his publishers as "prosperity writer extraordinaire," Murphy made a direct appeal to his followers' ambitions for wealth. His How to Attract Money, originally published as a fifty-two-page pamphlet in 1957, asserts in its promotional literature, "It is your right to be rich. You are here to lead the abundant life, and to be happy, radiant, and free. You should therefore have all the money you need to lead a full, happy, prosperous life." Murphy later published Riches Are Your Right (1958) and Your Infinite Power to Be Rich (1966). His subject matter was not limited to financial success, however; his themes ranged widely across the spectrum of Eastern and Western thought, drawing from both his personal studies of Divine Science and Asian religions and his formal education in clinical psychology. He discussed personal relations (Love Is Freedom, 1948), emotional serenity (Peace within Yourself, 1956); Asian divination (Secrets of the "I Ching," 1970), and the paranormal (Psychic Perception: The Magic of Extrasensory Perception, 1971). Of all his more than thirty books, nothing he wrote was more successful than the self-help manual The Power of Your Subconscious Mind (1963), which promises in its introduction to "lift you up from confusion, misery, melancholy, and failure, and guide you to your true place, solve your difficulties, sever you from emotional and physical bondage, and place you on the royal road to freedom, happiness, and peace of mind." An instant best-seller, it sold more than ten million copies in twenty-six languages during its author's lifetime.

Murphy toured widely in Europe and Asia, holding seminars on cruise ships and speaking to inmates at prisons as well as in the Church of Divine Science in Los Angeles. In time his congregation grew so large that he was forced to rent the Wilshire Ebell Theatre to accommodate it and to serve as the headquarters of the church. After his wife died in 1976, he moved to nearby Laguna Hills, where he continued to preach and write. In 1976 he married his administrative secretary, Dr. Jean Wright, a fellow Divine Science minister, who continued Murphy's ministry after his death until 1989. Murphy was a major figure in inspirational literature, combining spirituality, mysticism, and practical psychology in books that stressed personal development and self-reliance. Influenced in his thinking and writing by Ernest Holmes and other popular writers like Dale Carnegie (How to Win Friends and Influence People, 1936), Napoleon Hill (Think and Grow Rich, 1937), and Norman Vincent Peale (The Power of Positive Thinking, 1952), he was himself an important influence on later motivational writers and speakers.